Happiness:
A Lesson with Lulu™

Story ◦ Robert Jones
Paintings ◦ Anna Maddox
Arrangement ◦ Casey Marek

Healthy Life Press
Denver, Colorado

HAPPINESS:
A LESSON WITH LULU™

Copyright © 2018 by Robert Jones
Published by:
Healthy Life Press • Denver, CO 80219
healthylifepress.com
Author: Robert Jones
Illustrator: Anna Maddox
Designer: Casey Marek
Printed in the United States of America

Library of Congress Cataloging-in-Publication Data
ISBN 978-1-939267-74-0
BISAC: JUV033240 Juvenile Fiction:
Christian - Values & Virtues

Most Healthy Life Press resources are available wherever books are sold. Distribution
is primarily through Amazon.com and healthylifepress.com. Multiple copy discounts
are available directly from Healthy Life Press. Wholesale distribution of this book is
exclusively through IngramSpark.com and its affiliate, SpringArbor.com.

For every "Lulu"

-RJ, AM, CM

"Daddy," said Lulu, sticking out her bottom lip, "I'm feeling a little bit SAD today."

She slid under the covers on her bed.

"Why?" asked her daddy, lifting the blankets and peeking underneath. "I don't know," Lulu said quietly.

"How do I stop being SAD?"

"Hmm... What do we do when we don't know the answer to an important question?" asked Lulu's daddy.

Lulu popped out from under the covers. "Ask mommy?"

"I was thinking we would figure it out together," answered her daddy. "Perhaps we might find some clues at Sandpiper Sands?"

Lulu threw off her blankets and

B O U N C E D

around the
room...

so quickly that she
nearly took flight!

When they arrived, the rides were moving, the lights were flashing, and little feet were running in every direction.

"HOORAY!" shouted Lulu as she darted inside.

They twisted and turned through the morning.

Lulu's daddy could hardly keep up.

Afterwards, they unpacked a picnic lunch from mommy.

"This is the best day ever!" Lulu shouted.

Lulu's daddy smiled. "Do you remember
asking how to stop feeling sad?"

"Yes," said Lulu. "No one is ever sad at Sandpiper Sands!"

"Do you know that there are other ways to be happy?" asked her daddy.

"There are?" asked Lulu.

"Let's see if we can spot them from higher ground," her daddy suggested.

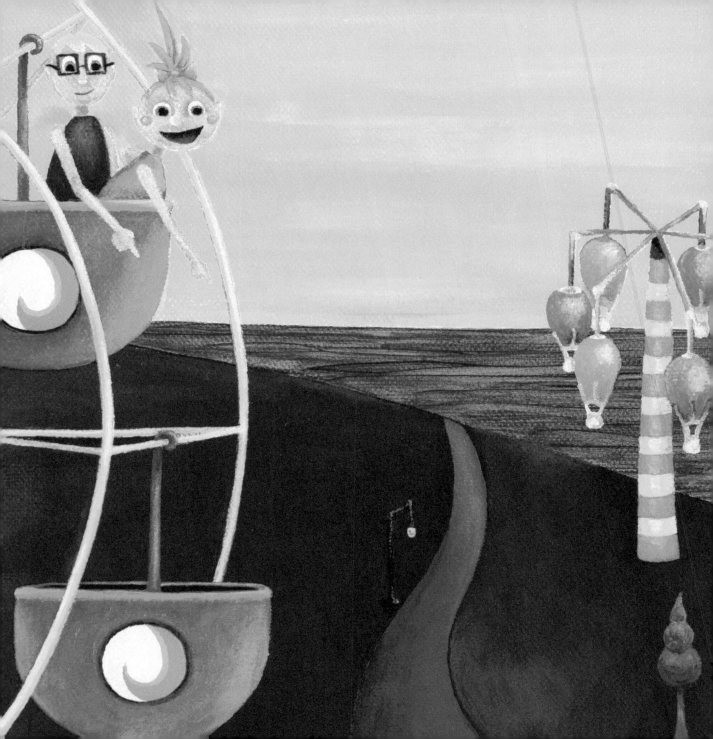

From high in the sky, they could see every corner of the park — the giant roller coaster, the hot air balloons, and even the ocean front.

Lulu's daddy pointed to a lady.
"She's coloring on that girl's face!" laughed Lulu.

"Do you think she is enjoying her work?" asked her daddy.

Lulu thought for a moment. "I think she is."

"You love to make things, don't you?" asked her daddy.

"Yes! Pictures and cards and toys and games and hideouts and breakfast and cookies and all kinds of things."

"I think we've discovered another way to be happy," her daddy said. "There's great fun in creating things, isn't there?"

Lulu was too busy trying to find happiness elsewhere in the park to reply. Finally, she pointed to a mechanic.

"Why do you think he's happy?" asked Lulu's daddy.
"He's doing important work!" Lulu said.
Her daddy smiled. "I think you're right. It's satisfying when we fix problems, especially when we're helping other people."

Lulu pointed to a boy who had just won a stuffed puppy.

"Why do you think he's happy?" asked her daddy.

"He did it! He won the game!" said Lulu.
"Great observation!" said her daddy. "I think we've found another way to be happy: achieving something you set out to do."

When she was done, the
little boy stopped crying and gave his
mommy a huge hug.
"Look, daddy!" said Lulu. "They are happy now!"

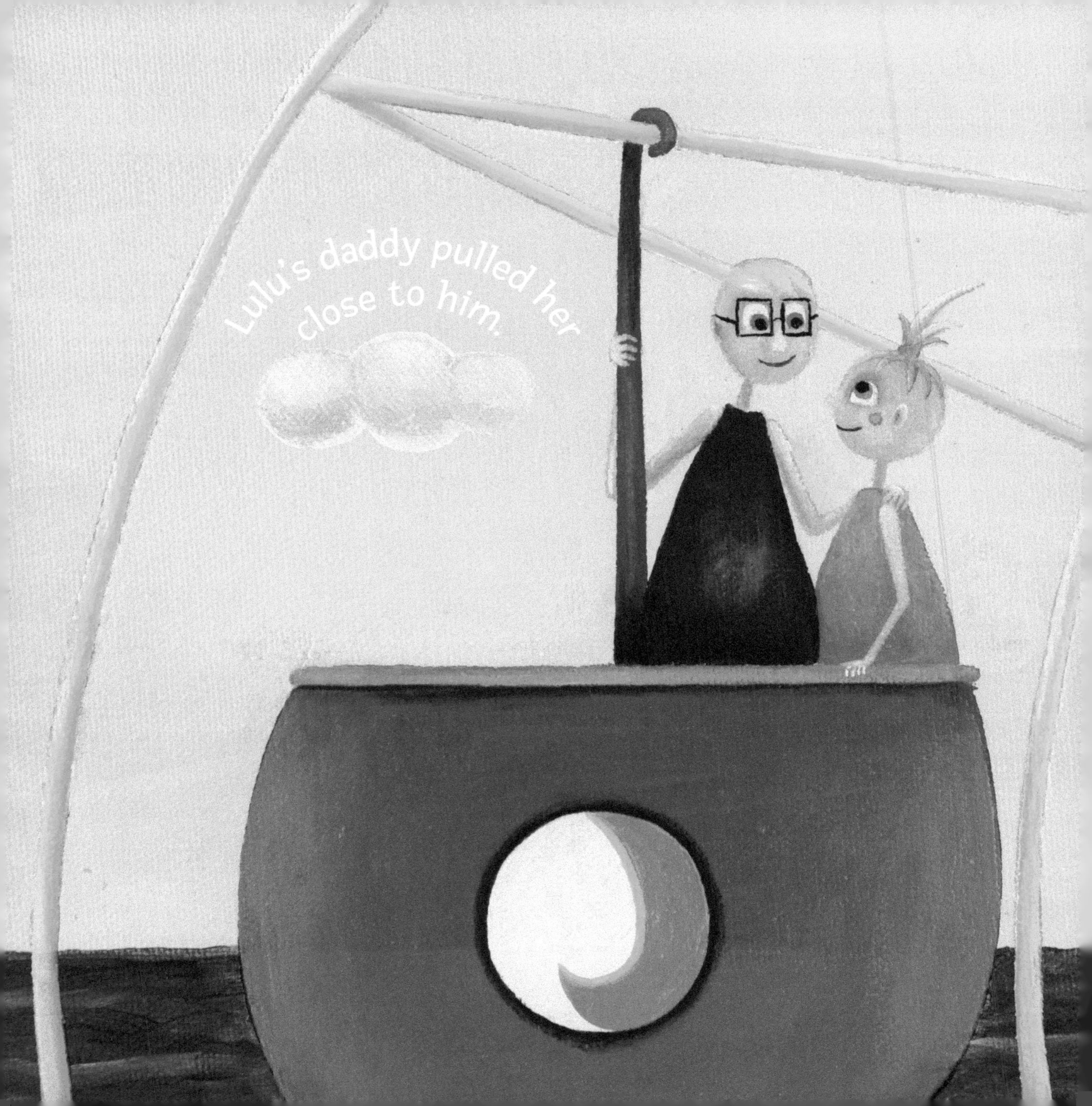

Lulu's daddy pulled her close to him.

"Life presents ever-changing situations, some pleasant and some not so nice. What matters is whether we approach each moment with an open heart and mind. When we do, every moment can be special."

"How do you do that?" asked Lulu.

"It takes practice," answered her daddy. "I'd bet the mommy was worried and upset. But she let those feelings go and with an open heart and mind, bent down and gently cleaned her boy's cuts so he would feel better."

"What about the boy?" asked Lulu. "What was he feeling?"

"I'm sure the little boy was surprised and in a lot of pain!" answered her daddy. "But he let those feelings go, and because he did that, he noticed all the loving care his mommy was taking with him. That allowed him to stop crying and feel better."

"Don't worry about any of your feelings," answered Lulu's daddy. "They are part of life. When you're hurt, it is okay to be hurt. When you're sad or angry, it is okay to be sad or angry. All feelings that spring up also fade away. When you let them go, you'll be able to see clearly and find the right thing to do. Your special light will shine."

Lulu gave her daddy a hug.

"Was that the right thing to do?" she asked.

"Well, I'm feeling happy," her daddy replied. "Are you?"

Lulu SMILED.

About the team

While miles apart, their stories share a beginning. Robert sat behind Anna in high school math class and watched her sketch pictures. Meanwhile, Casey was busy with arts and crafts in the elementary school next door.

Author

Robert lives in Atlanta, GA with his wife and two Lulus.

Anna is a civil engineer by day and artist by night. She lives in Nashville, TN with her husband and two naughty dogs.

Illustrator

Designer

Casey still likes to think of herself as a Lulu. She finds happiness through design, dance, and being pulled on walks by her ausiedoodle in Costa Mesa, CA.

HEALTHY LIFE PRESS
HELPING YOU TOWARD OPTIMAL HEALTH
WWW.HEALTHYLIFEPRESS.COM

AN INDEPENDENT SMALL CHRISTIAN PUBLISHER

CPSIA information can be obtained
at www.ICGtesting.com
Printed in the USA
LVHW07s0609030418
572039LV00003B/6/P

9 781939 267740